This book is for

HAVE FUN, MOLLY LOU MELON

written by
PATTY LOVELL

illustrated by
DAVID CATROW

G. P. PUTNAM'S SONS
An Imprint of Penguin Group (USA) Inc.

G. P. PUTNAM'S SONS
A division of Penguin Young Readers Group.
Published by The Penguin Group.
Penguin Group (USA) Inc., 375 Hudson Street, New York, NY 10014, U.S.A.
Penguin Group (Canada), 90 Eglinton Avenue East, Suite 700, Toronto, Ontario M4P 2Y3, Canada
(a division of Pearson Penguin Canada Inc.).
Penguin Books Ltd, 80 Strand, London WC2R 0RL, England.
Penguin Ireland, 25 St. Stephen's Green, Dublin 2, Ireland (a division of Penguin Books Ltd.).
Penguin Group (Australia), 250 Camberwell Road, Camberwell, Victoria 3124, Australia
(a division of Pearson Australia Group Pty Ltd).
Penguin Books India Pvt Ltd, 11 Community Centre, Panchsheel Park, New Delhi - 110 017, India.
Penguin Group (NZ), 67 Apollo Drive, Rosedale, Auckland 0632, New Zealand (a division of Pearson New Zealand Ltd).
Penguin Books (South Africa) (Pty) Ltd, 24 Sturdee Avenue, Rosebank, Johannesburg 2196, South Africa.
Penguin Books Ltd, Registered Offices: 80 Strand, London WC2R 0RL, England.

Published simultaneously in Canada. Manufactured in China by South China Printing Co. Ltd.
Design by Ryan Thomann. Text set in Stempel Schneidler Medium.
The art was done in pencil, watercolor, and collage.

Library of Congress Cataloging-in-Publication Data
Lovell, Patty, 1964– Have fun, Molly Lou Melon / Patty Lovell ; illustrated by David Catrow. p. cm.
Summary: When Gertie moves in next door with fancy toys and a huge television set, Molly shares lessons she learned from
her grandmother about homemade playthings and imagination. [1. Play—Fiction. 2. Toys—Fiction. 3. Imagination—Fiction.
4. Grandmothers—Fiction. 5. Friendship—Fiction.] I. Catrow, David, ill. II. Title.
PZ7.L9575Hav 2012 [E]—dc22 2011017587
ISBN 978-0-399-25406-2
1 3 5 7 9 10 8 6 4 2

Molly Lou Melon's toy chest overflowed with whoseywhatsits of all shapes and sizes. Her grandma had told her, "Back in the olden days, I didn't have fancy dolls or action figures. I made them out of twigs, leaves and flowers like hollyhocks and daisies."

So she did just that.

Molly Lou Melon's backyard had a big weeping willow and crumbly rock walls with thingamajigs peeking out from every crevice.

Her grandma had told her, "Back in the olden days, I didn't have a store-bought dollhouse. I made one in my backyard."

So she did just that.

Molly Lou Melon's garage was
full of colorful boxes and crates.

Her grandma had told her, "Back
in the olden days, I didn't have a race
car. I sat in a cardboard box and sped
down the hill."

So she did just that.

Molly Lou Melon lay on her
back in the tall, willowy grass.

Her grandma had told her,
"Back in the olden days, I didn't
have a television. I watched the
clouds that floated by and I saw
lots of things in them."

So she did just that.

One day, new neighbors moved in next door. When Molly Lou Melon went to welcome their little girl, she heard Gertie say to her mom, "I'm bored, bored, BORED!" Molly Lou Melon invited Gertie over to play.

On Monday, Gertie brought over her Darling Darla Deluxe Dollhouse complete with an electric mixer and working chandeliers.

Molly Lou Melon showed Gertie her tree root palace complete with acorn cap dinner plates, woven leaf air-conditioning system, and cicada Jacuzzi. Gertie was amazed.

On Tuesday, Gertie drove over
in her battery-operated fully loaded
Coupe de Ville.

"Look out below!!" Molly Lou Melon
screamed right before hurtling down the
hill in her turbo box car, hand painted with
orange and red flames. Gertie was amazed.

On Wednesday, Gertie was going to call Molly Lou Melon on her cell phone, but then she heard a strange sound coming from an old tin can that was dangling in her window.

"This is the operator, will you accept a call from me, Molly Lou Melon?"

"Y-y-yes?" Gertie spoke into the can.

"Great! Come on over! . . . Click."

Gertie was amazed.

On Thursday, Gertie asked Molly Lou Melon if she'd like to come over and watch cartoons on her big-screen TV. "It's 120 inches wide!"

Molly Lou Melon said, "Not today, thanks. I'm going to go watch the clouds. They're SKY wide!" Gertie was amazed.

On Friday, Gertie brought
over a homemade doll with
a frilly hollyhock skirt and
violets for hair.

"It's for your palace," she
said. And Molly Lou Melon
was amazed.

On Friday evening, Molly Lou Melon and Gertie were tired, tired, TIRED from playing all week. They lay down in the tall willowy grass, looking up at the clouds.

"I see a butterfly!" Gertie giggled. "And a penguin and a refrigerator!"

Molly Lou Melon opened
her eyes wide and grinned her
biggest grin. "I see a Grandma-
shaped cloud winking at me!"
And Molly Lou Melon winked
right back.